Tabby

Saves the Day

First published in the United Kingdom in 2005
by Chrysalis Children's Books,
an imprint of Chrysalis Books Group plc
The Chrysalis Building
Bramley Road
London W10 6SP
www.chrysalisbooks.co.uk

This book was created for Chrysalis Children's Books by Zuza Books.
Text and illustrations copyright © Zuza Books

Zuza Vrbova asserts her moral right to be
identified as the author of this work.
Tom Morgan-Jones asserts his moral right to be
identified as the illustrator of this work.

BRITISH LIBRARY CATALOGUING-IN-PUBLICATION DATA
A catalogue record for this book is available from the British Library.

ISBN 1 84458 481 X

Printed in China
2 4 6 8 10 9 7 5 3 1

Tabby

Saves the Day

Zuza Vrbova

Illustrated by Tom Morgan-Jones

CHRYSALIS CHILDREN'S BOOKS

Tabby always got her own way.
She could not remember a time
when she didn't.

5

Nobody argued with Tabby because
she was very, VERY good at everything.
She ran faster than anyone, she could skip
two ropes at once and she could climb up
the oak tree without any help.

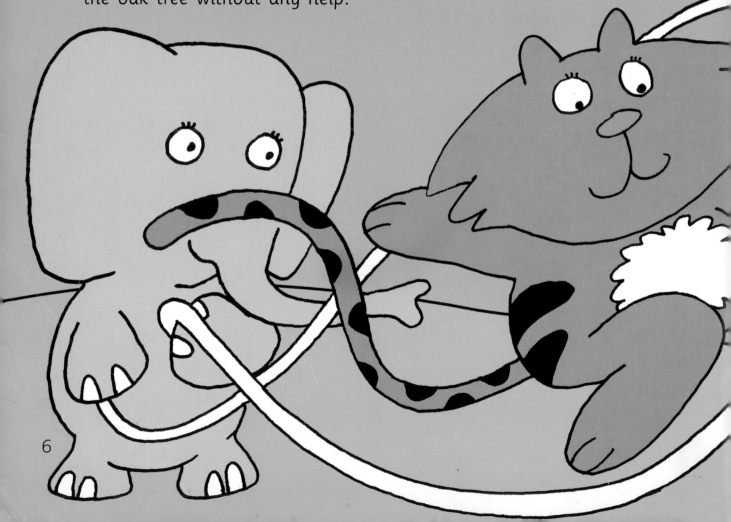

6

If Tabby couldn't do it, it wasn't worth doing.

She was also the bravest person in the class.

Every afternoon, on the way home from school,
all the children had to go past old Mr Price's garden.
Old Mr Price was grouchy and grumpy and
he didn't like children.

"Hurry up and move along, you lot," he would grumble
as Tabby and her friends walked past.

Ellie would clutch Tabby's arm. "Let's run, or he'll put us in a great big pot and cook us!" she would say.

"Don't be silly," Tabby laughed. "He's just grumpy and has bushy eyebrows. But he doesn't scare me!"

Tabby stopped by the fence and looked right at Mr Price.

"How are those roses then?" she said with a smile.

"Urrrumpphh," grumbled Mr Price as he always did.

"Oh, that's nice," said Tabby. "Have a good day."

And from that time on, Mr Price never said "urrrumpphh" again. That's how brave Tabby was and that's why no one ever argued with her.

But then one day, a new boy
came to school.

"Everyone, this is Bertie,"
said Miss Roo.

12

Everyone expected Bertie to be shy.
But he wasn't. He just looked around
and grinned. The classmates all felt
a little surprised. New kids weren't
supposed to be like that.

13

Right away, Bertie was different. He knew where all the continents were and how cars worked and how to add up huge numbers, just like that!

And, if that wasn't enough, Bertie could even skateboard! Backwards!

All of a sudden, everyone wanted to be friends with Bertie.

During football, they all wanted to be on his team.

And if Bertie said, "That's not a very good idea,"
Leo would say, "No, that's not a very good idea."

If Bertie said, "I like jam-and-banana sandwiches,"
Fred would say, "I like those too."

Tabby didn't understand why everyone suddenly wanted
to be best friends with Bertie. But it didn't bother her.
While everyone was trying to get Bertie's attention,
Tabby would read a bit more of her book
in her special place.

One day, Bertie said, "I have an idea! Let's go for a walk to the top of the hill!"

"Yes, let's," said Zoë.

"What a good idea," Fred agreed.

"We can climb the tree at the top," Bertie added.

So up the hill they went. The hill was steep and high, and the more they climbed, the farther away the top seemed to be.

"Won't it be very dark when we get back?"

Ellie whispered in George's ear. "What if we get lost?"

Fred asked, "How much farther is it?"

And Connie asked, "Are we nearly there yet?"

"It's OK. I know where we are," said Bertie boldly.
But Bertie was really thinking, I have no idea
where we are. We're lost!

When they reached the top of the hill,
there was no tree. The sky became cloudy
and it started to rain.

"I want to go home now," said Ellie. She was cold and was thinking about her dinner. (Ellie was always hungry.)

"Me too," said Leo.

"I wish I had my coat," said Connie.

All of a sudden, everyone felt a bit scared. They were lost.
And Bertie didn't know the way home at all.

Then they heard a yell.

"Hey, you lot. What are you doing up here?"

"That's Tabby!" cried Ellie.

"What are YOU doing here, Tabby?" they asked.

"I was reading my book in my special place,"
answered Tabby. "But I'm going home now.
Are you coming?"

"But we're lost!" they all shouted together.

"Well, help me pack my stuff and I'll show you the way,"
answered Tabby calmly.

"Do you know the way?" asked Bertie.

"Of course," she said with a smile. "I come here a lot."
Tabby took Ellie's hand and skipped along the path.
"Follow me!" she called to everyone.

Tabby smiled as she led them down the hill.

"Tabby, you are really VERY good at everything,"
Bertie said as they made their way home.

"She sure is!" everyone cheered.

Top of the Class

Collect them all!

Ellie Takes a Chance
Zuza Vrbova
Illustrated by Tom Morgan-Jones
1-84458-483-6

Zoë Wins the Race
Zuza Vrbova
Illustrated by Tom Morgan-Jones
1-84458-407-0

Piers Finds his Voice
Zuza Vrbova
Illustrated by Tom Morgan-Jones
1-84458-406-2

George Makes Friends
Zuza Vrbova
Illustrated by Tom Morgan-Jones
1-84458-482-8

Tabby Saves the Day
Zuza Vrbova
Illustrated by Tom Morgan-Jones
1-84458-481-X

Kit Paints the Sky
Zuza Vrbova
Illustrated by Tom Morgan-Jones
1-84458-404-6

Leo Takes to the Stage
Zuza Vrbova
Illustrated by Tom Morgan-Jones
1-84458-405-4

Roddy Learns a Lesson
Zuza Vrbova
Illustrated by Tom Morgan-Jones
1-84458-480-1

Visit the Top of the Class website at
www.topoftheclassbooks.com